Phonics Reading Program

BOOK 1
short a

Baby Jaguar Can!

by Quinlan B. Lee

SCHOLASTIC INC.

New York   Toronto   London   Auckland   Sydney
Mexico City   New Delhi   Hong Kong   Buenos Aires

Can Baby **Jaguar** climb
to the top of the mountain?
Let's climb with him
and Mommy **Jaguar**!
Grab the zip cord
and **clap** your hands.
Clap, clap, clap!

The wind is blowing **fast**.
Crash!
Oh, no! A tree fell on
the **path**.
How **can** we get **past** it?

We **can** swing on this vine.
We **can** swing **past** the tree.
But how **can** the **jaguars**
get **past** the tree?

Jaguars are **cats that can** jump high.
They **can** jump **past** the tree.
Can you jump like a **jaguar**?
Stand up and jump!

Can you see Baby **Jaguar**?
Jaguars can blend in well.
Look for **tan** and **brown**.
Can you find him?
No, **that** is a bird.

There he is!
Jaguars can run **fast.**
Can you run **fast**, too?
Stand up and run!
Run **fast, fast, fast!**

Baby **Jaguar**, jump to the top!
You **can** do it!
Let's **clap** and say,
"You **can** do it!"
Clap, *clap*, *clap!*

Baby **Jaguar can** get to
the top! Hooray!